A
Little
Bit
of
Love

JAMIE FERGUSON

BLACKBIRD PUBLISHING

A Little Bit of Love

Published by Blackbird Publishing, LLC
www.blackbirdpublishing.com

Cover design: Blackbird Publishing, LLC
Cover image: © Dmitry Remezov | Dreamstime
Interior design: Blackbird Publishing, LLC

Library of Congress Control Number: 2013953960

ISBN-10: 1939949041
ISBN-13: 978-1-939949-04-2

Printed in the United States of America.

For Maisie and Lucy.

Contents

A Little Bit of Love

JAMIE FERGUSON

First Dates

Julie tried to keep a straight face as Barry slurped his wine. It was their first date, and clearly — to her, at least — also their last. This had been a mistake. She should have known not to let Lisa set her up. But she had, and now she was on her first date in years, in a lovely restaurant, eating a wonderful meal and sharing a bottle of Barolo with a big, clumsy buffoon.

"So you sat on top of the washing machine?" he asked, then laughed. His laugh was a weird cackle that carried across the restaurant, as if a pack of geese had suddenly arrived. For a moment she thought he might start hiccupping as well — just like he had earlier, when she'd complimented him on his tie — but fortunately he didn't.

She'd just pretend she was having a good time. Like he was a nice, normal person she enjoyed spending time with. That would make it easier to get through the evening. Maybe.

"Well, yes." She smoothed the black lace of her dress and plucked off a stray bit of dog fur. "It wasn't balanced, or something, so when it hit the spin cycle it would move across the room unless I sat on it."

"It must have reminded you of having sex." He chuckled. A long, dark brown hair stuck straight up from his left eyebrow. She resisted the urge to kick him under the table. "I bet you really miss having sex, don't you? It must have been a while, since you're divorced and all."

Julie took a deep breath, then a sip of wine. If she said no, that would imply that she didn't enjoy sex. If she said yes, that would imply that she was a floozy. If —

What was she thinking? Was she actually going to treat this like a normal conversation?

She set her glass down, and the waiter refilled it. She jumped — she hadn't realized he was standing right there. He must have heard the entire thing. Oh my God.

"I think we've spent enough time talking about my household appliances." She brushed a curl out of her eyes. The waiter turned away and gave her a quick thumbs-up. Her embarrassment began to fade. Yeah! She thought. I handled that one well!

If only getting past that topic had been the last hurdle. If this guy hadn't been one of the managers at Lisa's company, she would have just bailed on the whole thing.

And yes, she did miss having sex. She liked having sex. And she'd thought Leo did too. Until he'd left her for George.

George.

How could you be in a relationship with someone for seven years and then decide you were gay? It wasn't as if she and Leo hadn't had sex. They had. Lots!

But one night last June, Leo had announced that he was leaving her for George. That he'd always been gay and "just figured it out now." Now, after seven years together.

For a while afterward she wondered if she too might be more interested in her own gender. That maybe, like Leo, she hadn't yet discovered her true colors. It was alarming. She'd get surprised by a salesgirl at the mall and would think: is my heart beating faster because I'm startled, or because I'm attracted to her? Because really, who knew?

But eventually she decided that she must be straight after all, and so when Lisa had pressed her, she decided to venture back into the dating world.

If tonight was any indication, it was a miserable world. It might be better just to get another dog and call it good.

Barry stabbed a tomato with his fork, jammed it into his mouth, and grinned. A piece of tomato was stuck to one of his front teeth.

At least the dog would have better manners.

"How 'bout football?" he asked through a mouthful of food.

Leo liked football. He and George had season tickets. They'd even invited her over to watch the Super Bowl.

"I don't care for the sport," she said. She had, but now it just reminded her of the past. She poked at her salad with her fork. One more course to go. Barry would want dessert, but she could probably come up with some excuse to squeeze out of that. Probably.

"Me either. Just on game days." Barry guffawed. He slapped his leg, shaking the table and knocking over her water glass.

The waiter materialized again. How did he always know just when to appear?

"I'll get that, Miss," he said, handing her a napkin.

Miss. He'd called her miss. She clearly wasn't a miss anymore; he was earning his tip tonight. Barry had damn well better pay it. She smiled at the waiter while he mopped up the spilled water and poured her a new glass. He was kind of cute — dark, curly hair, brown eyes. Like Leo, except taller, and with hair. And broader shoulders. And straighter teeth. And —

"Did you?" Barry interrupted.

Julie shook her head and realized she'd been staring at the waiter. He grinned at her and strode off. Was she so desperate that she'd moon over a guy she didn't know right in front of her date? Apparently. Or else it was her subconscious trying to help her keep it together for the remainder of the evening.

"I'm sorry, Barry, I was…lost in thought. What did you say?"

"I said, didja hear the one about the Polish priest who went into a bar?" He burped.

"Um, no."

Barry blathered on and she tried to make herself look as though she were paying attention. Maybe he wasn't such a bad guy. Maybe he just needed a woman's touch.

He burped again, then began to hiccup. Unfazed, he continued his story.

Maybe that could be some other woman.

And why was she on a date anyway? Did she even want to be in a relationship again? Was it worth it, putting your heart on the line, when the other person might change their mind at any moment? How could you trust them to not change, knowing that they could find someone else — George! — and stop loving you?

Leo said he still loved her, but as a friend. That he wanted to be friends. He'd been trying hard. Even her therapist was impressed.

This wasn't how her life had been supposed to go.

"I'm gonna take a leak," Barry announced. He pushed his chair back. Julie grabbed her water glass just to be safe. She watched as he walked to the men's room. He looked normal, from a distance.

The cute waiter appeared with two steaming plates of food. He raised an eyebrow at Barry's empty seat.

"Oh, he'll be back," she said. "Unfortunately."

"First date?" he asked. His eyes weren't brown after all; they were a warm amber. He had a light smattering of freckles across his face.

Julie sighed, then smiled. "Is it really that obvious?" That was good news. Imagine if she looked as though she belonged with Barry. Yuck. She ran a hand through her hair. She felt all jittery, as if she had been given a tiny break between aptitude tests.

"I've seen him here before." He chuckled. "He never makes it to the second."

Julie leaned forward and blurted, "I was married, but my husband left me for his golf buddy, and when we split up I got the dogs and moved to a new place and I like it, although I did paint the living room orange, but it all sucks and I didn't want to go on this date but my friend talked me into it and Barry is her boss' boss and —"

She broke off as she saw Barry heading back toward the table. Had she actually just said all of that to this poor guy? What on earth was she thinking? She pushed her wine glass away from her and stared at the table.

"It's okay," the waiter said in a low voice. "My name is Sal." He patted her shoulder, nodded to Barry, and headed off.

~~~~~

Barry walked back across the restaurant toward the table. This date was an utter disaster, just like they had all been. He didn't even have a successful dating past as a youth to look back on for help. He'd met his ex-wife at a party at his father's house, and things happened so quickly he didn't realize until after the divorce that it had all been choreographed ahead of time. How Ethel had been able to sleep with both him and his father all those years without either Barry or his stepmom figuring it out…now, that was some feat. A disgusting feat, but impressive nonetheless. Unfortunately, he'd had no evidence, so the courts had been less than impressed. At least he was finally done paying alimony and had enough money to go on dates again. A glutton for punishment, that's what he was.

And every time he went on a date it was nothing but punishment, although to save his life Barry couldn't think of a reason why the universe hated him so. Sure, he was doing well at his career, and even though he sucked at painting he picked up his paintbrush and dabbled every weekend. He ran every day, took yoga — hot yoga, no less, and he showered before and after to be more considerate. But there were no two ways about it. He was meant to be alone.

Take tonight. Julie, soon to be known as Failed Date #37. Her eyes crinkled up when she laughed. She was nice and sweet and funny and kind. And yet every time Barry opened his mouth he said something inane or idiotic or embarrassing. Or, more likely, all three. He'd even smiled at her with a big piece of tomato stuck to his tooth. Thank God he'd finally gone to the restroom and discovered that. And what had possessed him to make that comment about sex? It was as though once a date commenced his brain was replaced by that of a frat boy's, and all the real Barry could do was watch in mute horror at the ensuing chaos.

Barry's steps slowed as he realized the waiter was talking with Julie. Not again. That waiter had ended up dating five of the six women Barry had brought here on first dates. He probably would have succeeded with the sixth as well, except the busboy had gotten to her first. It was difficult to explain to a woman you'd just asked out that the restaurant she wanted to go to was off-limits because you couldn't compete with the wait staff.

He adjusted his cuff links as the waiter patted Julie on the shoulder. Barry took a deep breath and soldiered on to his table. As the waiter passed him they nodded to each other with masculine understanding. They both knew the score — Waiter: 5, Barry: 0.

For a moment Barry thought his hiccups were returning. He gulped and sat down, almost knocking Julie's water glass over again.

"I'm sorry," he said.

She shook her head and glanced in the waiter's direction. "No worries."

She was awfully pretty. Not the prettiest of the lot — that was #23, Beatrice. Beatrice the actress. Beatrice hadn't made it to dessert. He wished against all logic that Julie would. He really liked her. It was easier when he didn't like them this much.

Julie shook her head and drew her gaze back to him. She straightened her chair and took a small bite of food. Her movements were graceful, neat, and polite — unlike his jerky, big motions. Barry picked up his own fork. He'd try extra hard to keep himself under control for the remainder of the night. Everyone else seemed to be able to avoid acting like a bull in a china shop, so why couldn't he?

His fork fell out of his hand, bounced on the table, and landed squarely on top of Julie's plate of chicken.

Barry stared at her, frozen like a deer in the headlights.

The waiter appeared. "Looks like we had a little problem here. Don't worry, miss. I'll get the chef to whip up another." He whisked the dish away, leaving the two of them alone.

"It's okay," Julie said.

But it wasn't. Thirty-seven women had had to go through this horrible experience simply because they assumed he was capable of acting normal on a first date. God help the one brave enough to try to make it to the second. It was becoming quite clear that it wouldn't be Julie.

Barry felt a twinge in his stomach, like being in a plane that had just hit an air pocket. Dammit. He hadn't realized how much he liked her. But she deserved better.

And he was meant to be alone.

"No, no, it's not okay." Barry ran his hands through his hair. At least he had hair. For the moment. That would probably change soon enough. "I'm really sorry. I'm not a bad guy. I know I sound like a jerk. I just…"

~~~~~

"Hey Fred, gimme another chicken, on the double!" Sal yelled. He tossed the contents of the hot chick's plate in the trash, then dumped the plate into a bin of dirty dishes. It wouldn't be long, now. He just had to keep an eye on the girl in case she got so disgusted she stormed out of the restaurant, like Beatrice had.

"What's the matter, man? Losin' out on your new lady friend?" Fred chuckled. He grabbed a chicken breast and threw it into the grill pan.

"Dude, you have no idea." Sal grabbed a tray of salads for table #5. "It's that big loser who keeps finding me chicks."

"Ah, that guy. The ladies' man." Fred flipped the chicken and sprinkled salt on it.

"I'll be back in a minute. Make that one extra tasty; I'm in the homestretch!"

Sal peeked over at the new girl while he delivered the salads. She was *smokin'*. Her black lace dress was tight enough that you could tell she worked out a lot. As if he couldn't guess that by the muscle definition in her arms.

She wasn't loud and obnoxious, but quiet and refined. It was too bad that her dress wasn't cut lower, because he'd sure like to get a better look at that rack. That would come in time, though. Unlike the loser, Sal was a real ladies' man. It was that Italian blood of his. Like any good Italian man, he loved women. And they loved him. He generally only saw a girl for a little while before moving on, because who didn't like change? And it was time for some change. Sal was ready for another first date.

~~~~~

Julie eyed the glassware as Barry waved his hands in the air. She hoped Sal would hurry back so she could get this night over with.

"I just get so nervous when I'm on a date. It's like something takes over and I turn into a — a — a seventh-grade boy." Barry's hands dropped to the table with a thunk, making her jump. The glasses wobbled but remained upright. Julie let out a breath she hadn't realized she'd been holding.

Barry flagged Sal down and handed him a credit card. "Excuse me, could you please put this all on my card?"

That was weird. Why was he paying now? Although, at this point, nothing about this date should faze her.

Sal blinked. "Of course, sir," he said, and hurried off.

"I know I sound like a complete idiot. And I probably am one. But I just wanted you to know." He hung his head. "I'm sorry I said that stupid thing about you missing having sex. I'm sorry I got the hiccups. I'm sorry I had something stuck on my tooth. I'm sure I did more stupid things, so I'm sorry for all of them, too, whatever they were." He met her gaze. "You're a real nice girl, Julie. You're smart and beautiful and funny. You put up with a lot tonight, and I really appreciate you being so kind and patient. You deserve to be with someone more…together. Someone who isn't an idiot like me."

Barry lifted his hands off the table, which wobbled a bit but then steadied.

"I'm a bad date. Terrible. Please, accept my apologies for the whole thing. I know you said you were going to walk here from your place, but I can pay for a cab for you if you'd like."

Julie shook her head. "I'm okay," she mumbled.

Barry nodded. "Okay, then. Again, I'm sorry about the whole thing. Please have a nice life, and good luck with the waiter."

He stood up and smiled at her — a thin, weak smile — then marched out of the restaurant.

This was an unexpected turn.

Sal materialized. "Where'd he go?" he asked.

"Uh, he left."

Sal looked toward the door, then back at Julie. "I'm sure he'll come back for his card. He always does when his dates blow up. How are you doing?"

Sal was so cute. So nice. So understanding.

Julie smiled. Barry was…confusing. But this guy, he was more…straightforward. Normal. Predictable. She could use some normal after everything with Leo and George.

"I think I'm okay. It was a — a weird date." She hoped Barry was okay. Sal had said when his dates blew up, so this must have happened many times. How sad. The whole experience had been awful, but it was nice of Barry to apologize like that. She hadn't realized he'd been so nervous.

"Why don't I get your chicken wrapped up to go? Then maybe I can walk you home? Or we could go to the bar around the corner and I could buy you a drink?" Sal grinned. There was a dimple in his left cheek. "A pretty girl like you, all dressed up, well, you shouldn't put all that to waste."

What a charmer. He knew exactly what to say to a girl. So smooth, so easy, so relaxed. She'd enjoy herself with this guy. Right?

She could see Barry's head through the front window. He was trying to hail a cab, without luck. The poor guy.

What must it be like to be so nervous on a first date? She probably should have been more nervous herself. Maybe she hadn't been because she'd written Barry off within the first few minutes. Actually, to be fair, she'd written him off the moment Lisa had set her up. Maybe she, too, would have acted like a fool if she hadn't assumed the date would be a failure before she'd even met Barry. Maybe —

She plucked the card from Sal's fingers and trotted outside. "Barry, Barry!"

Barry turned around just as a cab squealed to a stop in front of him.

"Wait!" She ran up to him. "Barry, here — uh, you forgot your card." He was really quite attractive. And she hadn't noticed before how nicely dressed he was. Leo had always been such a slob. She handed him his credit card.

"Thanks," he said. He looked at his feet, then met her eyes. He smelled nice, like sandalwood and pine.

"Barry, um…" She twisted her hands together, then smiled up at him. "Would you like to go on another first date?"

Learning to Sail

The air was calm, there wasn't a cloud in the sky, the water lapped gently against the sides of the little sailboat…and land was nowhere in sight.

John stood on the fiberglass hull of the two-person craft and scanned the horizon. It felt as though icy fingers were running down his neck and back in spite of the fact that the temperature was in the upper 80s. He wiped his hands on his white T-shirt and squinted, first in one direction, then another. Maybe there…no, there to the left. No…

He balanced on the gently rocking boat for some time before conceding he was screwed. Utterly and totally screwed. He'd only closed his eyes for a minute, not nearly long enough for his boat to go out of sight of land. He'd been right off the island coast of Jost Van Dyke. Well, maybe a little more than "right off the coast." He'd gone further away from the Caribbean island in order to get out of earshot of yet another boat full of drunk, screeching college kids. Once he'd found a quiet spot, he'd been at peace for the first time in ages. He'd been alone. Away from people. Away from work. Away from technology. Away from any reminders of his crazy, stress-filled life.

He'd maneuvered himself into a reasonably comfortable position, sitting in the cockpit with his feet up on the hull, his head resting on his jacket. He'd stared up at the full sail, wondering if he should furl it, and then...

He'd woken up in the middle of the ocean.

Leaving the sail unfurled had apparently been a very, very bad idea.

John squeezed past the blue-and-white sail and sat down on the edge of the hull. He rummaged in the storage area in the back of the cockpit for the seventeenth time, but a GPS unit continued to fail to materialize. He'd made the brilliant decision to leave his phone in his hotel room so that he wouldn't accidentally drop it in the water. All he had was a life vest, a warm bottle of grape Gatorade, and a waterproof jacket. Other than the life vest, the safety equipment he'd been assured was in the boat was nowhere to be found.

He took off his flip-flops and wiggled his toes, then rested his head in his hands. Even if he knew what direction to head, there wasn't even a hint of a breeze. At least the sound of the water was soothing. If he weren't going to die at sea it would be quite pleasant. He closed his eyes and listened to the waves as they gently slapped the sides of the boat. *Slap. Slap. Slap.*

Something solid bumped into the port side with a soft thunk.

John jerked out of his daze and leaned over the hull, but there was nothing there but water. He'd felt something, though. Or had he fallen asleep again? He shook his head. He was stranded in the middle of the ocean because he'd taken a nap in his boat, and he'd been napping again?

He looked into the distance, but the line between the sea and sky remained a mere demarcation separating the two different shades of blue. He sighed and rubbed his eyes, then grimaced as the trace of sunscreen on his fingers made his eyes burn. Of course, that wouldn't be a problem for much longer, since he'd neglected to bring the tube of sunscreen. Pretty soon he'd be as red as a lobster. The tops of his feet already had that tingly, pre-sunburn feeling — except where the straps of his flip-flops had protected them.

He settled back down and wondered how long it would take him to die. A day? A week? He'd probably die of thirst before starvation. The thought made him thirsty, and he eyed the bottle of Gatorade. Might as well drink it all now and get the process over with sooner. He reached down into the cockpit and grabbed the warm plastic bottle.

"Hello."

He froze, one hand on the cap. The female voice was warm and mellifluous. He had to have imagined it — there was no one else for miles and miles. It seemed a mite early for it, but he was clearly going crazy. That might at least make dying of thirst a little easier. He set down the bottle and peeked over his shoulder just to be sure.

There was a beautiful woman floating in the ocean, her hands resting on the stern of the boat. She smiled up at him.

She had curly, dark brown hair that clung to her neck and to her bare shoulders, which was as much of her that he could see. Her eyes were a brilliant emerald green. The water droplets clinging to her skin sparkled in the sunlight.

"Uh. Hi." He ran his hand across his forehead. A mirage. That's what she was. His rapidly progressing insanity had created her to distract him from his impending doom. He scratched his chin. Perhaps going crazy wasn't such a bad thing after all.

"What are you doing out here?" she asked.

"I, um, fell asleep. When I woke up I was here."

She raised an eyebrow. Her eyelashes were long and dark.

"Have you ever sailed before?"

Great. He looked like an idiot to his mirage. His face grew hot.

"Yes, but it's been a while."

He refrained from mentioning that 'a while' was twenty-three years, that he'd been a kid at the time, and that almost everything he'd done today he'd only known to do because he'd looked it up online before leaving the hotel. He hadn't lied to the boat rental place — he really did have the required 30 hours of sailing experience. He just didn't remember most of it.

"What's your name?"

"John."

She surveyed him for a moment. Her hair was drying in the warmth of the sunshine. Tiny little curls had sprung up around her forehead. The larger curls seemed full of energy, almost as if they were alive.

She took a deep breath and hoisted herself up onto the boat. She wasn't wearing a top.

John stared at her wet breasts as they were jostled about by her movements, then pulled himself together and scooted to one side of the boat so that she had enough room to sit. He dragged his eyes to meet hers, but they quickly wandered back to her torso. She wasn't real, so it wasn't rude. Right?

He was so distracted by her breasts that it took him a moment to notice her bottom half.

"Hey, what the —?" He pulled away from her, lost his balance, and barely managed to keep from falling overboard.

She grinned and smacked her tail fin against the hull. The motion made her breasts bounce, as if they too were happy.

From the waist down she was a fish; her tail stretched out across the top of the little boat. Her scales were a rich green with hints of gold. They shimmered in the sun. Water dripped off her fishy half into the cockpit and pooled in a small puddle on top of his jacket.

"Eirene." She held out her hand.

John took it cautiously. Her skin was soft and smooth. Should he shake her hand? Kiss it? What was appropriate when meeting a mermaid? He tried to surreptitiously peek at her middle, where the human and fish halves converged. The transition was very swift, a band of tiny scales that changed rapidly from green to flesh-colored, then became skin.

"It's, uh, it's a pleasure to meet you, Eirene." His eyes kept wandering back below her navel. It didn't seem too disturbing, not after the initial shock. Having a tail looked right on her, somehow. Which made perfect sense, since his imagination had created her. Could she really turn her tail into legs, like in the myths?

She squeezed his fingers, then released them. She didn't smell like a fish, but of the ocean breeze by the shore, salt and sand with a hint of seaweed. He had an almost uncontrollable urge to touch her scales. Would it feel like touching a fish?

"You're a long way from the islands," she pointed out.

"Yeah, I know," he muttered. He fiddled with the hem of his T-shirt. "I didn't plan very well."

She tilted her head and looked at him as if she were taking his measure. A light breeze sprung up and tousled her hair. The boat began to move slowly as the wind tugged gently at the sail. It could be going in the right direction. Or not.

"I'm usually much better prepared for everything," he said. He wiggled his toes and stared at the sail. "I'm just so tired. I work too much, and it never stops. Never. There's always one crisis after another. I'm only here because the CEO decided he wanted to have a meeting on St. John, but it's a total boondoggle for the executives, and the rest of us have work to do. I've spent every day this week on the phone and trying to keep my laptop online, but the network connection at the hotel sucks. This morning I just couldn't take it anymore, and I rented this boat. Which was obviously a stupid idea, since now I'm in the middle of the ocean and I'm going to die here and the only good thing is that I'm going crazy and my imagination came up with you."

He stopped babbling, took a deep breath, and gave her a sideways glance. He licked his lips; they tasted of salt and sunscreen.

Eirene looked up at the sky. Her hair was almost completely dry now. It hung well down her back, and a thick lock covered the nipple on her left breast. His eyes wanted to focus on the right nipple, but he forced them up to her face. Her mouth was pursed, as if she was thinking about something. The more he looked at her face, the more he wanted to keep looking at it instead of her more curvaceous bits. He found himself hoping she'd turn toward him so he could look into her eyes again. The breeze tugged a small chunk of hair across her face, and he found his hand lifting to brush it away. She tossed her hair back into place with a shake of her head and he yanked his hand back, hoping she hadn't noticed.

"What, uh, what do mermaids do all day?"

She turned to look at him, and he cringed. This was starting to feel like a bad date, where every time he opened his mouth he said something more stupid than the last.

"I mean, do you just swim around and look for sailors who are lost?" Yes, this was exactly like a bad date. He clamped his mouth shut and tried not to look as dumb as he sounded.

She chuckled. Her laugh was warm and infectious. He would have enjoyed it more if she hadn't been laughing at his ineptitude, but he couldn't help but smile.

"You're an exception." She poked him in the arm. "Besides, most people who sail actually know how."

There certainly was no arguing with that. His skin tingled where she'd touched it.

Eirene waved at the vastness of the ocean gliding by past them. "There's so much to do. We're stewards of the sea. We help the little creatures. Especially these days." Her eyes narrowed. "Humans are destroying the earth. So, no, I don't normally help people who get lost because they don't know how to sail."

He swallowed and glanced up at the sky. The sun was behind them, and the wind had picked up a bit. They were making decent time, if only further out into the middle of nowhere.

"I avoid eating fish that's overfished," he said. "But I can stop eating it altogether."

She rolled her eyes. "Don't be silly. Fish are tasty. Although at least you're paying attention to what you shouldn't eat."

John felt a brief moment of happiness at having done something she approved of, then noticed her expression, which made it clear that there were plenty of other things he'd probably failed to do.

"The problems are much bigger than what you eat or don't eat." She rubbed a spot on her — leg? What was the right term? It didn't seem to make sense to call her entire bottom half a tail. Her scales had dried, and he wondered how long she could go without having to get them wet again. "Even if you never ate fish again, the ravage of the oceans would go on."

John bit his lip and tried to think of a response that would help make up for the fact that he spent most of his time sitting in front of a computer instead of campaigning against environmental destruction.

Nothing sprang to mind.

"You're right," he said finally. "The problem is big. Way bigger than me, or than you. Even though you are a mermaid," he added hastily. "I don't know. I'm sorry humanity is stupid. We're destroying other parts of the world too, not just the oceans. It's not fair. I'm really sorry."

She studied him for a moment. He felt as though he'd just taken a test that he'd forgotten to study for. But it didn't matter. He was going to die out here anyway. She wasn't even real. And even if she had been real then he would have deserved to feel bad, and probably die too, because he was human and therefore apparently part of the problem. He hung his head and stared at the pale white stripes on the tops of his feet where his flip-flops had been.

"I like you, John," she announced. The smile that brightened her face was like the sun coming out from behind the clouds after a weeklong rainstorm. He found himself smiling back.

"I like you too, Eirene. I'm sorry you're not real and I'm going to die of thirst out here. I would have really liked to get to know you better." Trite, but accurate.

She squeezed his arm.

"Are you always this much of a pessimist? We merfolk never stop finding ways to have fun." She grinned. "And that doesn't mean sitting around all day combing our hair."

She shielded her eyes and looked at the sun, then back at him.

"Turn to starboard," she directed.

"What?" He blinked. He must have missed something.

"The boat. I want you to turn to — to the right." She giggled. "I could tell that you didn't know anything about sailing when I found you asleep so far from land. Do you know how to turn the boat?"

"Uh…" He tried to remember what he'd seen in the videos that morning. "Yeah, you pull this thing. The uh —"

"No, you don't. And that's called the tiller. Here, hold the — this thing. And pull this — hey, not too hard or you'll tip the boat over!" Water splashed over the hull and into the cockpit, drenching them both.

Fortunately the little craft wasn't going very fast, or it would have capsized. His morning studies were starting to come back to him, although it was clearly a good thing that Eirene knew more about sailing than he did. They both ducked out of the way of the boom as it swung around. The sail billowed and the boat picked up speed as it headed on its new course to wherever they were going.

Eirene scooted closer and snuggled up to him. He put his arm around her and rested his hand on her scales. They were soft and warm, nothing at all like the skin of a fish. One of her nipples was pressing against his chest — he could feel it through his now-soaked T-shirt. He swallowed and tried to concentrate on her hair, some of which had twined its way around his neck, like an aquatic form of ivy.

"Hey, is that land?" he asked. There was a faint smudge on the horizon. He blinked, but it didn't go away. Eirene wrapped her arms around him. The island grew larger and larger. They sat in silence as the white dots in front of it began to look like miniature boats.

"Is this all real?" he asked. He grabbed her shoulders so he could look her in the eye. "Are you really real?"

"Don't I seem real?" she replied, and squeezed him. She retrieved her hair from his neck and waist.

"I'm not going to die, and you really are a mermaid?" The back of his neck prickled.

She smiled and moved to the edge of the boat, then flipped her tail over the side.

"Wait! Don't go!" He reached out and touched her arm. "Please don't go."

"I can't stay here," she said. "I can't allow myself to be seen."

"But — but I'd like to see you again. Can I?"

Eirene ran a finger over her lips, then leaned over and kissed him. Electricity surged through his entire body, like he'd just grabbed a hold of a live wire. She pressed her lips to his ear.

"The fifth of May, at the lighthouse in San Diego."

She slid off the boat into the water, and vanished.

"Wait!" he yelled, leaning over the side of the boat. There was nothing there but the ocean.

John scanned the water, but she was truly gone. He turned back toward shore, wondering which island he was approaching.

The sunlight sparkled on something in the cockpit; it was one of Eirene's scales. He stared at it for a moment, then put it in his pocket.

What had she said? San Diego in May? May fourth. No, the fifth. He was supposed to go to a conference in Boston that week, but his job had sucked away enough of his life. Perhaps it was time to make some changes.

And to take some sailing lessons. Just in case.

A Good and Honorable Thief

Stagecoach robberies didn't end up with people being killed, just robbed. Eliza had read about them in the newspaper back home in Philadelphia. No one had ever died during a holdup by road agents.

As far as she could recall.

Eliza could hear the road agents talking to each other through the open window of the stagecoach. She tried to concentrate on what they were saying, but couldn't make out their words. Her insides felt all fluttery, and she was breathing like a horse after a hard run. She scrunched her eyes closed and tried to settle herself. She was always the calm one — her sister Corinne was the one who panicked, who cried or fainted at the drop of a hat.

"We should have taken the train," Eliza muttered. She tugged on the pale green cotton muslin of her skirt, some of which had gotten stuck underneath the large man sitting to her right.

"They won't finish laying the tracks for at least another year," her sister Corinne whispered, her blue eyes full of fear. Her grip on Eliza's left arm was so tight it was starting to hurt. "As if that matters now anyway! We'll be lucky if we don't get shot!"

Eliza rolled her eyes and tossed her hair over her shoulder, narrowly avoiding smacking her sister in the face. Of course they weren't going to be shot. Just stripped of all their valuables. Fortunately they had virtually none after having to pay off the debt Father had left when he'd died.

She peered past her sister and out the open window. All she could see were low, scrubby bushes, and beyond them grass-covered plains, with snow-capped peaks far off in the distance. The June air smelled like sagebrush and horses.

Eliza rubbed at one of the many dirty spots on her dress. The West was a dusty, filthy, wretched place. She knew she should be grateful that Uncle Alexander was taking them in, but he'd set the condition that they had to make this horrible trek and move to San Francisco. As if there was any other option.

So here she and Corinne were, crammed into a stagecoach with seven other passengers — with a handful more sitting on the roof — being held up by bandits in the middle of the endless nowhere called Wyoming.

"The only thing that would make this worse would be if Indians showed up," Eliza muttered under her breath.

"Don't say that!" Corinne exclaimed, then clamped her hand over her own mouth. Her eyes darted around. One of the men in the row in front of them turned around and glared at her. Corinne grabbed Eliza's arm, her eyes as wide as saucers. "That's in the stagecoach company's rules! You're not supposed to talk about In — about them!"

"We're not supposed to talk about robbers either, so should I not mention the fact that we're being held up by some *right now*?"

The well-dressed man sitting in front of Corinne looked over his shoulder at them, his countenance stern. "Would you young ladies please be quiet? The more you chatter, the more likely the road agents are to take notice."

Eliza pressed her lips together and nodded. She twisted a finger in the silver chain of her necklace. The blue stone that hung on the end of it lay hidden under the fabric of her dress. The necklace was the only token Eliza had left of their mother, who had died seven years ago, a week after Eliza's eleventh birthday and three days before Corinne's ninth. Corinne had a brooch of Mother's that she'd pinned onto the inside of her skirt so that ruffians wouldn't see it, which was probably wise given the calamitous nature of their journey. Eliza released the chain and patted it back down under the collar of her dress.

"They'll be takin' notice soon 'nough," the Southerner sitting in front of Eliza said in his funny drawl. He'd said he was from South Carolina, or maybe it was North? He patted his holster. It seemed like every man in the West carried at least one firearm. Which might not be a bad thing today, although the bandits wouldn't really shoot anyone. Would they?

It felt as though it had been hours since they were stopped, but in reality it had only been a few minutes. Maybe they weren't being held up at all. Maybe the driver had taken a nip too many from that bottle he was always lugging about and had decided to frighten his passengers.

"Everybody out of the stagecoach!" a man's voice ordered.

Eliza's heart thumped. They truly were being held up after all. This was *real*.

"Everyone on top of the coach, get down here now. Those of you inside, get out. And keep your hands up! We'll shoot every man who puts his down!"

The carriage jostled as the people riding on top climbed down. Eliza wondered how they were managing to do so while keeping their hands in the air. The men inside the carriage exited, leaving the two girls huddled together.

"What should we do?" Corinne asked, her eyes wide.

"I suppose we'd better join them," Eliza replied. A bead of sweat trickled down her forehead, and she rubbed her face against her sleeve. She scooted across the seat and slid out of the coach onto the ground. Corinne followed, somewhat less gracefully.

Two scruffy men dressed in leather and brown cotton stood pointing rifles at the collection of passengers. One was middle-aged; the other was an older, weathered man with a scraggly gray beard. Another man was pulling things out of the baggage compartment. All Eliza could see was the back of his balding head. Two more men stood off to the side, their handguns by their sides, clearly at the ready. One was young, maybe in his early twenties; the other had hair as dark as a raven's. The stagecoach driver was nowhere to be seen. She hoped he wasn't injured, or — God forbid! — dead. He was an awfully irritating man, but still.

"Hand over your arms, please," the younger man said. His tone was polite, as if he'd just asked someone to pass a plate at the dinner table. His face was kind and warm. He was wearing a shirt made of animal hide, like an Indian would. He was tall, with strong, broad shoulders.

He tucked his long, dark brown hair behind his ears and began collecting revolvers from the male passengers. He examined each one, then carefully placed it in a rough, earth-colored sack. He really was quite handsome, if you could ignore his odd attire.

His eyes met Eliza's, and she realized she'd been staring at him. She bit her lip and looked away. She could feel her cheeks burning.

The Southerner eased his hand down toward his holster. A shot rang out. Corinne grabbed Eliza's arm. Eliza swallowed. Dust curled up from the ground in front of the Southerner.

"That there was just a warning," the dark-haired man said. Smoke curled up from his gun.

The young man collecting weapons looked at the girls, an expression of concern on his face. He glanced at the smoking gun, then went back to his chore.

"Y'all can consider me warned," the Southerner replied. Even with a rifle pointed at him he sounded like a lazy summer day.

"And we do." The black-haired man's mustache was fuller than his beard, so his face looked rather top-heavy. He was wearing a blue coat so worn it was hard to tell for sure, but it seemed awfully similar to the uniforms Eliza remembered from the war.

The two girls huddled together while the gun collector finished his task. The only sounds were of one of the passengers clearing his throat, and the incessant buzzing of the flies. Lord, there were an awful lot of flies out here.

The young man carried the sack over to a tree and set it down. It bulged with weapons. A lot of good they'd done. Really, what was the point of carrying a gun out here if the ruffians could just pluck it away?

The leader made a quick, sharp gesture. The other two riflemen stepped back, their guns still trained on the passengers.

"Jake, get their valuables," the lead ruffian ordered.

"Yes sir, Captain," the young man replied. He retraced his steps, but this trip was far less fruitful. It seemed guns were more plentiful than jewelry among the passengers. He acquired a small amount of money, a pocket watch, two rings, and a gold chain that took a moment to get untangled from one of the passenger's surprisingly long chest hair. Corinne averted her gaze during the process; Eliza knew she should too, but she was unable to tear her eyes away. She hoped she'd tucked Mother's necklace all the way under her collar, but was afraid to check lest she draw attention to it.

The baggage searcher, finally finished going through all the luggage, walked over to join the gunmen. Eliza glanced at him as he passed by, then gasped as she recognized the bald pate — it belonged to their driver! He had colluded with the robbers!

Prickles ran down her back as the leader lowered his gun and sauntered over to them, his steps slow and steady. Eliza snapped her mouth shut, wishing she hadn't made a sound when she'd recognized the driver.

"What have we here?" His voice was deep and rough. The driver and the man with the gray beard chuckled. The man collecting jewelry glanced over at them, then continued his task.

Eliza stood up straight as the ruffian approached. Corinne's grip on her arm was so tight she was surely going to have a bruise, but the way the leader was looking at them she'd be happy if that was the worst that happened. He wouldn't hurt them. He wouldn't.

"Perhaps we should take a little more…treasure…" He reached a hand out and touched Corinne's cheek. She whimpered and pressed her face into Eliza's shoulder.

Eliza met the man's eyes. They were icy blue, and cold as a creek full of snowmelt.

"We don't have any jewelry," Eliza lied. She lifted her chin up high and tried not to wrinkle her nose at the scent of body odor. He smelled even worse than the men she'd been jammed in with for the past few days.

"I'm not talking about baubles. I'm talking about you two young, nubile women." His eyes moved down Eliza's body, then back up to meet hers. The corner of his mouth twitched up in a crooked smile, and he nodded. Eliza felt as though he'd just looked through her clothes and seen her in a way no one but the man she married should see her. She tore her eyes away from his face.

His jacket was missing most of its buttons, but this close up it was clearly part of a uniform. Had he really been a captain during the war? All the officers Eliza had known, both during the war and afterward, had been gentlemen – which this man clearly was not.

"We're not going with you." Eliza's voice was firm and clear in spite of the fact that she felt as though her knees would buckle at any moment. "Our father di — died, and we're going to live with our Uncle Alexander in San Francisco. He owns a hardware store."

As if this horrible man was going to listen to her. He wouldn't really kidnap her and Corinne. He wouldn't. He couldn't. Oh, if only Father were here! *He* would have been able to figure a way out of this awful dilemma.

"I believe your travel plans have changed, missy." He reached a grimy paw out and touched the side of her face. His shirt was grimy, as if he'd rolled in mud and then put his jacket back on over top without bothering to even try to clean himself off. Eliza took a step back, dragging her sister with her. The man chuckled. "You're coming with us. I've been a bit…lonesome."

Eliza's eyes darted back to the passengers, but they were under gunpoint. They couldn't help her and Corinne. No one could help. She swallowed and squeezed Corinne's shoulder.

"Captain?" It was the young man, Jake.

The captain turned to look at him. "What is it?" His voice was sharp.

Jake set down the bag he'd been putting valuables in. "I'm sorry, sir. This isn't right."

The huddle of passengers growled in agreement, but stopped when one of the road agents pointed his gun at them.

"Right or not, that's the way it is. *My* way." The captain grinned at Eliza. One of his front teeth was missing. "And don't worry. You'll get a share. There's two o' them, and I'm a man who don't mind sharin'." He winked at the girls. Even from several feet away he smelled of whiskey.

Eliza felt as though her insides were being squeezed by a wringer. No self-respecting man would even *say* these things to a woman!

"Some officer you are!" The words poured out of Eliza as if a spigot had been opened. "My sister and I helped out during the war. We sewed buttons on uniforms, and sat with the injured. Every man we met was good and honorable. Unlike you."

The captain raised an eyebrow at her. "I'm glad we've run into such patriots." He turned to his men. "Let's load up," he said. "And we're taking these girls."

Eliza's ears were ringing as though she'd just been knocked on the head. This couldn't be happening. It just couldn't be real.

A fly landed on her shoulder, making her jump. It buzzed away. She put her arm around her sister. Maybe she could talk him into taking her and leaving Corinne. Maybe. She shivered in spite of the summer heat.

Eliza steeled herself, opened her mouth, then closed it as Jake took a few steps toward the captain and the two girls.

"I don't believe we are, sir." His voice was as solid as an oak tree.

"What did you say?" The captain ran his hand through his hair and eyed the young man. "Did I just hear you counter an order?"

Eliza caught her breath as she realized Jake's hand was on his gun. The captain glanced down and noticed it as well.

"Respectfully, sir, that's not an order I can follow."

The captain shook his head, his eyes not leaving Jake's.

"You're asking for trouble, boy." The captain's expression was as hard as a stone wall.

"I'm sorry, sir."

The two men stood, unmoving, for what seemed like forever.

Eliza shivered. Should she run? They'd surely catch her. And she couldn't leave Corinne. What could she possibly do? She felt like an animal caught in a snare. Her heart thumped so loudly everyone must surely be able to hear it.

"Sir, we've followed you for a long time. Things have been awfully tough since the war ended. But this is going too far."

The captain glared at Jake. "*I* make the decisions."

"Yes, yes sir, you do. Stealing because we're starving and desperate is one thing. Hurting innocent people is another. We had to do things during the war that none of us are proud of, but we did them out of honor. There is no honor in this."

The other road agents looked a bit unsettled.

The captain spat on the ground. "I'm your commanding officer, Lieutenant. You do what *I* want."

"Cap'n?" one of the other road agents called. "Cap'n, I, uh, this might not be the right thing to do. We don't need them fillies. And we certainly don't need to do anything that would get the cavalry after us."

"Yeah, I don't want to be meetin' no cavalry boys," another said. "Maybe you true blues do, but I deserted to stay *away* from the military."

The captain's narrowed eyes didn't leave Jake's.

"I'm sorry, sir." Jake's voice was soft. "The war is over. Things are different now."

"I'm still in charge." The captain's voice was low and dangerous. "And don't you forget it."

"Yes sir." Jake stood straight as an iron post.

The captain looked at Jake for a moment, then turned to the rest of his men, his voice loud and boisterous. "Alright, men. Let's get this wrapped up and get on our way. Jake, see if these girls have anything that we *can* take with us. Besides, I'd rather spend my time with a lady who knows the ropes, if you know what I mean."

Several of the robbers laughed. Two of them moved into the bushes and brought out their horses.

The captain turned to look at Jake, his eyebrows raised. After a moment Jake nodded, then moved in between the captain and the girls.

"My apologies, Miss. Do you ladies have any jewelry?" he asked Eliza. His eyes were a warm, rich brown.

Eliza's gaze flickered over to the captain, then back to the young man. He smelled earthy, but not in a bad way. Maybe it was the hide he was wearing. She shook her head. If she opened her mouth she knew she'd burst into tears.

"I can see her necklace from here, Lieutenant." The captain's voice was harsh.

Jake's eyes didn't leave Eliza's. "I'll need your necklace, if you don't mind."

Mind? Of course she minded! It was Mother's necklace!

But there wasn't any choice.

Eliza extracted her right arm from under the press of Corinne's body, undid the tiny silver clasp, and handed it to the man. She held her hand out for a moment, the necklace tight in her fist. She dropped it into his palm, her fingers brushing lightly against his skin. She pulled her hand back quickly; it was warm where their skin had touched.

He held her necklace in his hand for a second, then gave her the briefest of nods and dropped it in his bag. "I have it, sir," he said.

The captain motioned to his men and they began to move back, their guns still trained on the passengers. He turned back to Jake and muttered, his voice low, "I'll remember this, boy."

"I understand, sir," Jake replied.

Eliza stood as still as a rabbit as she watched the road agents move out of sight into the bushes. She stood until the sound of hooves faded, then she wrapped her arms around her sister as Corinne began to cry.

~~~~~

May was a busy time at Uncle Alexander's store, so the sudden lack of patrons in mid-afternoon was like a cool breeze in the summer. Eliza sat down on the stool and closed her eyes, then sighed as the bell on the front door jingled. Corinne had been no help since she'd met that dandy of hers. All she did at work was wander around blathering about how wonderful he was. She should be back from the market soon, and then at least Eliza could take a break and hope that Corinne paid at least a little attention if a customer showed up.

Eliza pushed herself to her feet as the man who had just come in took off his hat and approached the counter. His short, dark brown hair was parted on one side.

He nodded. "Good afternoon, miss." His voice was low and warm.

"Good afterno —" She froze in mid-sentence. He wasn't — was he?

A chill ran down her back as she recognized the young man from the stagecoach robbery last summer. Uncle Alexander was out back for a bit, and wouldn't hear if she cried for help!

"Don't worry," he said quickly. "It's only me."

"Only *you*?" Eliza's voice sounded like the squeak of a little mouse. "That's why I'm worried!" She looked around, but Uncle Alexander failed to magically appear.

He adjusted the collar of his wool suit and looked down at the ground. She wondered if he preferred the Indian shirt. "I guess that didn't sound so good. I'm sorry, miss. I don't mean to frighten you."

He lifted his head and met her eyes. He was even more handsome than she remembered. Her face grew hot, but she couldn't pull her gaze away. How on earth had he managed to find them? Eliza vaguely recalled babbling about going to San Francisco. He must have remembered that.

"I'm alone," he said. "I'm not with my — the other men in that party anymore."

Eliza swallowed, then squared her shoulders. "I should hope you're not carrying about with those ruffians anymore. Although you're not any better yourself."

But he had stood up to the captain. She felt her heart patter as she remembered how she'd watched his fingers rest on his gun. She hadn't forgotten what he'd done. Would he have shot the captain to save her and Corinne?

Jake twisted his hat in his hands. "After the war we didn't have anything, no food, no way to get to where we'd come from. Just the clothes on our backs. I didn't have any home to go back to anyway. Our house was burned to the ground during the war, and my parents and sister…they didn't make it out. So when the captain headed out west, I went with him. I didn't realize we'd end up so desperate to survive that we'd become robbers." He took a deep breath. "I left them after we stopped your stagecoach. That's not the kind of man I want to be."

Eliza blinked at him, unsure what to do, what to think. It must have been awful when he discovered what had happened to his family.

He then pulled a small leather bag out of his pocket. "I came to return this to you."

He upended the bag on the counter and shook it lightly. Eliza gasped as Mother's necklace poured out, the blue stone shining like the blue of the sky outside. She reached out to touch it with a shaking finger.

"Mother's necklace! Oh, thank you!" She grabbed it and beamed at him, feeling joy radiating from her being. He smiled back. She put the chain around her neck, her fingers fumbling with the clasp. Then Eliza remembered he was a ruffian, and her expression turned as cold as iron.

"You should never have stolen it in the first place. But thank you for returning it."

His face was sober. "You're most welcome. I — I'm sorry about what happened. I hope both you and your sister are well."

Jake touched the brim of his hat, then turned and walked toward the door, his boots clicking on the floor. His wide, strong shoulders looked just like they had last summer, when he had stood in between them and the captain.

He had been a thief, but he had saved them from what surely would have been a fate worse than death. He'd disobeyed orders and stood up to the captain to save her and Corinne. And he had brought her necklace back. He must have stolen it from the captain.

"Wait!" she called. He stopped, then turned slowly around. She leaned forward, over the edge of the counter. Her heart thumped so loudly he surely must be able to hear it. She took a deep breath.

"Could — would — would you come back tomorrow?"

His face brightened, like the sun coming out from behind the clouds.

"It would be an honor."

About the Author

Jamie Ferguson lives in Boulder, Colorado, where she spends her free time attempting to tire out her two herding dogs. Her first novel, *With Perfect Clarity*, was published in 2013.

www.jamieferguson.com

www.ingramcontent.com/pod-product-compliance
Lightning Source LLC
Chambersburg PA
CBHW071214130626
46555CB00004B/1706